# TL;DOCAMERON

## Twisted Tales for Turbulent Times

### BARRY KELLY

The manufacturer's authorised representative in the EU for product safety is
Authorised Rep Compliance Ltd, 71 Lower Baggot Street, Dublin D02 P593 Ireland
(www.arccompliance.com)

Troubador Publishing Ltd
Unit E2 Airfield Business Park,
Harrison Road, Market Harborough,
Leicestershire. LE16 7UL
Tel: 0116 2792299
Email: books@troubador.co.uk
Web: www.troubador.co.uk

ISBN 978 1836282 327

British Library Cataloguing in Publication Data.
A catalogue record for this book is available from the British Library.

Printed and bound by CPI Group (UK) Ltd, Croydon, CR0 4YY
Typeset in 11pt Minion Pro by Troubador Publishing Ltd, Leicester, UK

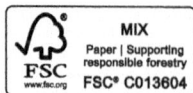

MIX
Paper | Supporting
responsible forestry
FSC® C013604

*To Mum and Dad: thank you.*

# CONTENTS

# PREFACE

In the year 1348, a group of ten young worthies escaped courtly Florence and The Black Death to shelter – or "lock down" as we would have it – at a secluded and vacant estate in Fiesole. Over the course of a fortnight, by way of entertainment, each was charged with telling ten diverting stories. Allowing for holy and household duty days, this left ten days to recount their tales: ten days, ten people, 100 stories.

This then is the premise of Giovanni Boccaccio's masterpiece, *The Decameron* (Ten Days), published in 1353. Written in the Florentine vernacular, it is a cornucopia of timeless tales, perhaps a Tuscan *Arabian Nights*: universal yarns that touch us all.

In 2020, history repeated itself, as we remember all too well. A malevolent new microbe appeared, in the distance at first, but ever advancing, pernicious and deadly. The Nobel Laureate Peter Medawar described a virus, as indeed it was, as "a piece of bad news, wrapped up in a protein". This tiniest of specks, arguably not even alive until it meets us, came as an awful warning. Masters of all we surveyed, or so we thought, we were paralysed by the most ancient of maladies.

Tipping my hat to Boccaccio's past triumph, I wondered if I could ape the enterprise. Quarantined, my fictional author, closeted in his solitary cottage, sat down to write some stories. These would all be in different styles and voices. I hoped that within these, I might stumble upon my own. Being a medical man, I couldn't resist a slight alteration in title: hence *The Docameron*. His patron, The Laird, an expert on, among other matters, prime numbers, encouraged him to ignore the decimal element and simply "blatter on, laddie!"

With apologies to Boccaccio and indeed world literature, I humbly offer these offerings to the court.

*Barry Kelly*
*Belfast, 2024*

# THE LAIRD: FOREWORD

It was a soft autumnal evening as I crunched my way from my bothy up to the Laird's castle. I had been here as his house guest for many weeks. I passed the days lost in my labours, writing paused only for the simple quotidian needs of food, drink, sleep and the occasional summons to see The Great Man. This was such an occasion. Reaching the immaculate gravel drive that led to the castle, I paused a moment. The magnificent grounds swept away in every direction. On a far-off hill, I saw the great stag, Dougal, silhouetted in the gloaming. Locals claim that as long as Dougal guards these craggy peaks, peace will reign. For a second, I could have sworn that the fearsome antlers dipped towards me, as if to say, "Aye, laddie, ye may pass – this time. But I'll be watching ye closely, ye ken?"

When I arrived, I found the Laird sitting in the ancestral hall, bagpipes on his knees. His eyes had that faraway look I associated with composition. Doubtless another haunting masterpiece was taking shape in that amazing mind. Mechanically, his fingers flexed and extended as they ran up and down the chanter at a speed that was both breathtaking and, I must admit, a little frightening.

As I entered, he turned towards me, his sapphire-blue eyes scanning me. He nodded gravely and, the salute of the ruler thus bestowed, with a twitch of his left eyebrow he motioned me to sit opposite him upon The Great Oak Visiting Chair. This, I did, smiling gratefully. Nothing was said for some time as he continued his internal musical fugue, somewhere far, far away.

I surveyed the room.

On the walls, noble ancestors gazed, and occasionally glared, from their places of veneration. The history of this place, extending back over hundreds – thousands – of years, some said, was all too easy to see in their noble visages.

My eyes fell first upon Hector, the thirteenth Laird, with his Glaswegian wife Senga; then Aengis The Mystic, the fifth Laird resplendent in his plaid kaftan; and the tenth Laird, Ruairi the Ruthless, named in part because of his warlike nature but mostly because his betrothed, Ruth, had absconded with a bicycle salesman from Pitlochry.

Ah yes, those had been dark days indeed. Even now, bicycles are frowned upon by the Laird of the day and on each anniversary of that fateful event The Laird still officiates at The Great Frowning wherein an ancient rusting two-wheeler is dredged from the estate's lake. The entire household then encircles it and wags a collective finger in admonishment, while the Laird reads suitable incantations from The Clan Reciter.

I've never seen the ceremony myself of course, but locals have whispered that for days afterwards, any cyclists within twenty miles of the estate mysteriously become disorientated, dizzy and find themselves dismounted and staring in bewilderment at their machines' slowly deflating tyres.

In the east portico hung the portrait of Douglas, the eighth Laird. Douglas, an early and thrifty proponent of organic food, was said to have worn his stays to the point of flitters, at which time he simply boiled them with oats, a little honey and a wee dram, and fed them to his more blithely ensconced houseguests. Thus, went the legend, it could be unwise to outstay one's welcome. No pun intended, presumably.

Next to Douglas was the fourth Laird, Sandy: Alexander Avalon de Courcey Benedict, to be exact. Sandy had always been a Europhile, hence Benedict, the Patron Saint of Europe, I surmised. Sandy had traveled widely, collecting tapestries and, some said, "nieces" although others claimed that this had simply been a mistranslation of "Nice', a city which had embraced Sandy like no other. In fact, the clan beret (he had refused to call it a bonnet), worn subsequently on ceremonial occasions at a rakish angle, completely covering the right ear, was one of Sandy's great contributions to this hallowed place. The family motto, "l'Écosse, C'est Moi!" was another. For a time back in Sandy's day, French had become the language of The Court. Eventually this would revert to Gaelic, with French reserved for high table only (and, some muttered, the Laird's *lettres*).

In front of the fire, two enormous hounds lay sleeping. The only sound was the rhythmic ticking of a clock on the massive oak mantlepiece. The Laird stirred again from his reverie and leaned forward towards me.

"So, laddie, ye've been in ma bothy all summer. What have ye tae show for it?"

"Well, Laird, I've written some short stories."

"Have ye now," he answered, setting down the pipes and picking up a glass from a small table next to him. He sipped The McUisce, his own 83-year-old single malt. (The Laird was also an authority on both distilling and prime numbers.) "Have ye, indeed."

He poured me a dram and handed me a tumbler along with, as was his custom, a sprig of fresh moss. I raised the glass in acknowledgement.

I nodded. "Yes, Laird."

"What are they about then, mon?"

"Well," I began, lowering a mouthful of The McUisce, "that's the thing..."

"*The Thing*?" he barked, eyebrow arched, glass poised and the stare now more piercing than ever.

"Er, yes," I hesitated. "They're all different, Laird. They have nothing in common."

"Huh. I see, laddie," he snorted, considering this answer carefully. "Like a tin of shortbread biscuits. Except of course," he conceded, "for the shortbread," he chuckled, savouring his own bon mot.

"Exactly so, Laird."

He removed his beret and scratched his head thoughtfully with his ceremonial *hairdirk*.

"I expect it's just yer strange Hibernian ways," he growled.

"I fear so, Laird," I whispered.

"Tell me laddie, have ye brought them wi" ye?"

"I have indeed, Laird," I stammered and fetched them from my battered satchel.

"Hmmm."

He set down his tumbler on the oak table with such force that Hamish, one of the two hounds, momentarily leapt up, mistaking it for the command to hunt, or at least maim.

"Easy there, big mon," soothed The Laird. Thus reassured, Hamish returned to his doggy slumbers.

The Laird leaned towards me.

"Right now, laddie" he said, accepting the bundle. "Away wi' ye then. I've some reading tae do."

# GAIA

You were asking me about the house? Yes, well of course we've had it in the family for generations. It's remote, as you can see, alone on the edge of this cold, deep lake. Beyond the lake, dark mountains stand jagged against the sky. Funnily enough there's always snow at their summits. Or perhaps I imagine there is. I'm getting older, you see. The mind plays tricks.

Anyway. I am talking too much. Please, come in.

Now, to the left just inside the door, you see an assemblage of coats, hats, slippers and shoes. It can be challenging up here and it's best to be prepared, especially against the cold. We now find ourselves in this lovely small hallway. To the left, there are two bedrooms: one green and one blue. There are bunk beds in one room and a single bed in the other. Beyond that, there is an airy blue room with the most wonderful light. A round window overlooks the lake. The sunlight is perfect in the morning, somewhere between butterscotch and lemon pie. I love both, you see, so I can never decide. Outside, the lake breathes life into its hinterland, season by season. In summer, the diving birds appear. Swooping from somewhere very high they dive into the lake and disappear again. They say the beak is very sharp and not to be reckoned with. I certainly wouldn't like to be on the receiving end of it.

Next, let me take you to our living room – a beautiful space with views of the same lake, as you can see. Sometimes I perch by the window if no-one is around and simply gaze out. The beauty never fails to move me. Perhaps the word is "majestic". Does that sound right? There are bookcases everywhere and the books are about everything. I like a room full of books, don't you? I think books speak of open minds and tolerance. Over there you can see the wonderful brick fireplace facing the window. When it's lit, sitting by the fireside is the most comforting feeling: to be warm and safe, especially when the wind is shrieking outside and the snow is swirling.

The kitchen leads off the living room and always catches the evening light, if there is any. It's delightful there too. Warm, with wonderful smells, constant bustling, cooking and, well, joy, I suppose. The fridge is over there to the right of the window and the range faces it. How we love it when it warms us. What is it about food? It seems to involve so much: crockery, bread, cheese, butter, the clattering of knives and forks and the promise and reward of a full stomach.

We live in the attic. We are snug here although it can be very cold in the long winter. We do what we can to stay warm. The wind comes howling in from the lake and if I'm honest, it sometimes frightens us.

We've been here for years, guarding our people. We watch over them from above when they come to visit us.

They can be very noisy in the evening, but I love that. The house becomes alive. We hide in our attic, listening, knowing that we will have food at some point – some morsel that they don't notice. They laugh, sing and celebrate each other, almost exactly the same way that we do. From my perch, I can see them outside skating on the frozen lake in winter or boating in the summer. In the evening, I can hear the little ones laughing in their beds when they should have been asleep. We are seen only rarely.

Some time ago, I first had a conversation with one of them – the lady who painted these lovely flowers on the cupboards. Well, to be accurate, I was curled up hiding in a dark corner watching her, but she was definitely talking to me.

"Don't hide away there, my little friend," she said. "Come over by the fire and let me see you."

I walked towards her – nervous but trying to look brave. She bent over and whispered, "I'm not really here, you know."

I hesitated. "Are you..." I paused, looking for the right word "– a ghost?" She smiled. "Yes, I suppose I am." She looked at me out of the corner of her eye. "Are you afraid?" I shook my head, laughed and said, "No. Are you?"

"No," she said firmly. "Some people might but I'm not, my little mouse." So, we both sat in front of the fire in the silence. "I love it here," she continued, raising her eyebrow in my direction. "It's perfect. When they are all here, I think my heart may burst with happiness."

"Why?" I asked.

"I love it, don't you see, because they're all here. All my family are with me and I love them all so much."

I looked up towards the attic and nodded, "So are mine, and I do too." She glanced down at me, stroked the back of my neck and said, "Why, of course you do."

We often have such interesting times, she and I. When there is no-one else here, I perch on the arm of her chair and listen as she tells me stories. Such adventures she and her family have had here! I curl up and drink it in. Occasionally she will stroke my back absentmindedly as she tells me a tale.

"Do you have a husband?" I asked her on one occasion. She was silent for the longest time, gazing into the fire, lost somewhere else far, far, away. Finally she looked at me and smiled wistfully.

"I loved him very much," she answered with a sigh. "He died before me but luckily we are together again. He was 'The One', you see." I nodded, and of course, I felt the same. "When we first met, the timing wasn't right, I suppose. So, we waited for years until it was, and we could be together." I nodded again. "Then we had our children and they all came here, eventually with theirs. Such bliss it was."

She sighed and was silent again for a long time. I could see shiny tears sliding down her face. When I asked her why she was crying, she said that it was with happiness. She grieved when she couldn't be here, in this holy place. I told her that I was sure she would always be here, looking after them and us.

She always painted everything so beautifully. Hour after hour she had created a world but only a few would ever find it. I believe she did that deliberately. You can feel it, can't you? The spirit of the house? Only a few could see that she was sending herself into their future. A balm for tomorrow: a sanctuary for the wounded soul. We believe in souls too, you know. Ah, you didn't know that? Yes, we do.

She told me that she adored painting beautiful blues, yellows and reds. So many flowers.

She would often sing to herself when the others were away. Her singing is always here, or at least I believe I can always just catch it, even when I can't quite see her. Everywhere here. You only have to close your eyes and listen. No, listen. She is here. Ah, lovely. You can hear her? Well then, this might be the perfect place for you. Not everyone can hear her, but I believe that she planned it that way. The house will choose you. Others have told me that they just couldn't find it. I mean, it's hard to miss, isn't it? It's almost as if the house is hiding from them. Then again, it's a place in which to love and be loved, to be healed, to be in touch with the past and the future through the wind and the water. To be shaped by the power of that which we can't see or touch but can feel – that same elemental joy that binds us all, if we would only let it.

I apologise. I'm being too philosophical. But the world outside can be very distracting and it is easy to miss the deeper truth. Yet you only have to close your eyes and that truth, and this house, will find you and you will find it. I just know you will.

# FLATMATES

There it was again. The sound of splintering wood and falling masonry informed Cuchulain his flatmate had returned. "Another door off its hinges," he sighed. "That's going to need repaired." Even though he had expected it, the solid impact of a dead cow on the kitchen floor still shook him. A mighty spear thudded into the wall. Inwardly, Cuchulain groaned wearily.

"Good evening, my brave old friend!" bellowed Finn MacCool pleasantly, tossing his boots into a corner and then casually picking at something interesting he'd noticed in a webbed space between his toes. He sniffed it, momentarily interested, then flicked it casually into the fire. This was to be expected.

"What are you up to?" Finn asked. Cuchulain raised an eyebrow and considered whether or not this question was genuine and required any actual answer. On balance, he thought he would acknowledge it, "I'm working on my new range of clothes and jewellery."

"Really?" replied Finn in a far-off voice, casually eyeing the array of woollen balls, semiprecious stones, blackthorn and silver on the table. "Yes," continued

Cuchulain tentatively. This was interesting: an acknowledgement. He could never be sure if Finn had actually heard what he had said or even was capable of comprehending it. Although some people had claimed that MacCool was a bard, capable of reciting mellifluous poetry (apparently), he himself had never witnessed this and remained sceptical.

Feeling optimistic, Cuchulain pressed on. "I have decided to call the collection Cloak and Dagger." He turned and looked in MacCool's direction, noting without surprise that Finn had become suddenly distracted by something else. Whistling something unrecognisable and, to be honest, slightly painful, he had begun stripping the hide from the unfortunate beast. This he did with speed and relish. "You have to give him credit," Cuchulain thought. "He is damned good at that."

Pausing in his labour, Finn realised that somewhere peripherally in his world, a conversation had been going on and as far as he could recollect, it was likely that some response would be required. Yes, that struck a chord somewhere. "Erm, very interesting," he replied, pronouncing each word carefully as if he were handing over coins in a currency with which he was not familiar to a shopkeeper in a faraway land. Which, in a real sense of course, he was.

"You never take any interest in my life," muttered Cuchulain petulantly. Finn considered this. He thought hard. He had registered Cuchulain's tone and was fairly sure it indicated there might be clouds on his horizon. "That's not fair, I've been out all day hunting. Look what I've brought back!" he bellowed, proudly, indicating the carcass.

"Hunting?" disdained Cuchulain.

"Yes!" roared Finn. "I have been out hunting with The Great Men of Erin. Over many hills and dales, we rode. Many's the mighty river we forded, myself and The Great Men of Erin. Many's the fearsome creature we had to dispatch, and many were the –".

"Spare me," sighed Cuchulain. Finn looked genuinely perplexed. He had begun his tale enthusiastically and was determined to finish it. "Many were the wild beasts that blocked our path, but they were no match for The Great Men of Erin."

"Here we go," thought Cuchulain and let him get on with it. Finn recognised this as an opportunity and, planting one boulder-sized foot on the battered sofa, continued his recounting.

"Yes, I shall relate further. Although the sun baked us, the rain lashed our faces and the wind tore the cloaks from our backs, we, The Great Men of Erin, would not be diverted from our task. Pausing only to engage in discourse with the bards, delighting as we do in reciting the great poems of Erin, and to spear the mighty fish from the deep wild rivers of our great green land…"

As he spoke, Finn's eyes sparkled dreamily like the jewels on the Cuchulain's table. In his reverie he was elsewhere, reliving the adventure.

"This could go on for hours" thought Cuchulain. "Did you get the avocado and coriander? Did you remember that we have people coming tonight?"

Finn fumbled in the pocket of his sheepskin jerkin, a garment the size of a tent but yet stretched tightly across his massive muscular frame. A shovel-sized hand retrieved a crumpled piece of paper. He unfolded it and great gobs of mud and God knows what else dripped from it.

"Read. The. List." hissed Cuchulain, massaging his temples. "Read the list," Finn repeated.

He focused on the unfamiliar words, "avocado, coriander, salmon (not farmed!), harissa sauce and meringue nests." He frowned. What in the name of the Great Red Bull of Ulster was a meringue? What class of flying thing could that be? He, Finn, the greatest of all warriors in all of Erin, had seen, and truth be told, killed one of every kind of bird in the land. Could it be the great eagle? The hawk? The mighty kestrel? He looked inquiringly at Cuchulain. Cuchulain faced him, his arms folded and his legs crossed, and stared back blankly.

"Am I correct in thinking that you haven't actually brought back anything on that list?"

"Indeed I have, my great friend!" exclaimed Finn gesturing proudly at the now hide-free heifer draped decorously across three chairs. "My share of the hunt, slain this very day by myself and the great warriors of Ireland."

Cuchulain swivelled around in the general direction of carcass. Finn took this as approval and continued. "This handsome beast will sustain us through the long winter nights ahead, my friend." He folded his massive scarred hairy arms and sat back, supremely satisfied. He even allowed himself a wink and nod, secure in the knowledge that surely now he must be on safe ground.

"What are we supposed to do with it?" Cuchulain asked slowly and deliberately.

"Why, I shall build a great spit, worthy of the beast, and we shall feast, drinking ale and recounting stories of the..."

"Let me guess," interrupted Cuchulain, "The Great Men of Erin?"

"Indeed!" thundered Finn, slapping a hand on a thigh the size of a tree trunk. His laughter rattled the windows.

Cuchulain indicated towards the beast. "And how do you think we're going to get that into the oven?"

Once again, the great warrior was confused. Surely, he thought, a spit was the way to go here. For the great warriors of Erin, it had always been a spit and thus it should always be. Instantly lost again in reverie, he recalled all those unforgettable nights when the great warriors of Ireland sat around their campfires after a long day's hunting, roasting their bounty, their cloaks pulled about them and their great boarhounds at their feet as they told stories of the great warriors. "Mostly about me, to be fair," he conceded modestly.

"I will do it," sighed Cuchulain. "I will get the shopping, including the meringue nests."

"Hmm, those nests again," thought Finn. He put his left thumb into the great cave of his mouth and pondered. Presently something stirred, deep within his cranium. Something important. Something to do with birds. Something about birds and his old mate. Ah yes, he remembered.

"Watch out for the crows!" he shouted as Cuchulain wrapped a stylish mauve cloak tightly about him and fastened it with a finely wrought silver broach, one of his own. "Crows?" "Yes, old friend, crows. Definitely crows."

Cuchulain rolled his eyes, scowled and slammed the door behind him. "The man's a total legend," laughed Finn. "But I mean, Cloak and Dagger? Seriously?"

# ABYSS

Oblivion. Well, it had seemed like oblivion but for how long he couldn't say. Now if someone asked him, he would say that it was a really peaceful experience, here under the water. Swimming? Was he swimming? No, that wouldn't be accurate. It was more like drifting. Looking up he could see the light. It looked gorgeous. Musical. Was that the right word? His rational self informed him that it couldn't be so. Yet it was musical, vivid, psychedelic. As he approached the surface he was saddened, but in the gentlest way – nothing to worry about at all – as that embracing oneness faded slowly away. As he floated to the surface, his senses became more defined. The world fell into focus. He felt the cold sea suddenly penetrate him, stabbing him everywhere, rejecting him. "You must leave this place," he thought he had heard it say. How odd.

Dimly he could make out shapes in the water around him, noises now too – the roar of the ocean and somewhere, he wasn't sure exactly where, a panicky raspy breathing. Wasn't that someone crying? Where had that come from? Yes, he was sure it was. A man. A grown man sobbing. He looked around, still underwater, but saw no-one. Yet as he swam up the crying was getting louder. His eyes opened as his face left the water, warming suddenly as he felt the warm sun on his face.

He was amazed at how quickly his clothes dried, and miraculously soon were loose and fresh. A little salty water left his mouth. He coughed momentarily as a little more came up. He shook his head groggily. Christ, he'd never been much of a swimmer. He focused as best he could, still aware of the whiskey in his system. Its effects were slowly evaporating.

On the beach, he picked up the bottle, almost full. Bushmills single malt. Beside it was its cap. Carefully he twisted the cap on; calmly, slowly. A discarded blister pack lay next the bottle.

He despised litter and the people who left it. Always a tidy man, he bent down and examined it carefully. Diazepam: 10mg. Most of the blisters had been opened and the contents were missing. He scanned the horizon, again suddenly overcome with sadness. No-one visible. Suddenly he didn't care. Litter was the least of the world's problems, or his. The more he thought about it, this, this stupid pack of tablets, the more incomprehensible it seemed that he should ever have cared about it, this place, his world.

Panicking, he closed his eyes and thought of those he loved – who loved him. His wife, who would be frantic now and his three children. He forced himself to concentrate. To remember happiness. A memory flickered inside. Holding his youngest baby daughter minutes after her lengthy entrance into the world. The smears of his darling wife's blood on the baby's white downy little body. Momentarily he felt, yes actually felt, her nascent hand curl instinctively around his little finger as grinned his boyish smile at her. 'His boyish smile', that's what his wife had always called it. He raised himself from his knees and stood, stooped and lost. How had he gotten down there, and, bereft as he certainly was, noted with his clinical acumen still intact, how light he must be now, to have stood up so quickly.

He walked back to his car. It was the only one in the car park. The door was unlocked and, he was appalled to find, the keys still in the ignition. He shook his head in despair and climbed in. He slid the whiskey bottle into an empty plastic bag on the passenger seat and placed the blister pack carefully in his jacket pocket. He looked in the rearview mirror and reflexively straightened his tie. As an afterthought, he glanced up again into vacant, red, swollen eyes staring back: pitying him, despairing at him, jeering at him. He looked at himself for what seemed like an age, feeling nothing. The emptiness was total. There was no possibility of escape. Not this time and how he had tried. He took a deep breath and glanced at his wretched, pointless, useless, embarrassing, worthless self, one last time. He started the engine, and as he did so, he felt it coming again: a wall of pain. Without warning he began to cry. Loud, undignified, unmanly, almost animalistic noises pouring from him. "Maybe I can still feel something?" he whispered, emphasising the last word and spitting each out in angry syllables as the tears formed at the corners of his eyes. "Just something." He was begging the universe, his God. No answer came. The decision made, he checked his side-view mirrors, his rear-view mirror, released the handbrake and drove slowly and carefully out of the car park.

# YERCRAZIUM

"Right, mate? Flippin' Baltic the day, like."

I replied politely in the affirmative; succinctly but I hoped affably that indeed his meteorological diagnosis was accurate: inclement with the glass close to zero but given the season, events we must "weather" with due and apposite stoicism.

"I'm getting a bus for to see The Mucker, like," he continued.

Nodding, I agreed that as a conveyance and well-established mode of public transport, the omnibus was rightly, highly regarded. Peerless, even. We stood at the bus stop in amiable silence, stamping our boots as one does in that time-honoured tradition to dissipate the cold and demonstrate our undying conviction that these small bursts of kinetic energy would in that great way of the laws of thermodynamics provide heat and therefore solace; in the podiatric environs at least.

"Aye, he's sent for me, you see. The Mucker, like."

I nodded non-commitally in acknowledgement, smiling at my fellow traveller. I then returned to my private reverie and my quotidian task of recalling verse learnt in quondam days. Today's was *The Lay Of The Last Minstrel* from the great pen of Sir Walter Scott. Closing my eyes, I began to recall those first lines: "In peace Love tunes the shepherd's reed; in war he mounts the warrior's...."

"Oh aye. The Mucker's been workin' at the fishin'. He's asked for an assistant, like. You know, for the easier bits."

I averred that since the days of Izaak Walton, and possibly long before, angling had often been seen as a metaphorical and possibly metaphysical struggle between man and nature and moreover could readily appreciate that extra assistance is often welcome at critical junctures. I did venture that this current month, February, did not seem the optimal time for riverbank sporting pursuits.

"Eh?"

"Angling," I repeated. "It's a heroic time of the year to be fishing."

"Anglin'?" He seemed confused.

"Yes, angling. You know, as in fishing?"

"Ah no," he laughed. His pitying eyes told me that my perceived idiocy required rectification. "*Fishin'*," he emphasised, as though addressing a simpleton. I confess that I was a little nonplussed and definitely none the wiser. Perhaps the terms were not entirely synonymous but were generally considered to intersect.

"I'm afraid I don't under–" I started hesitantly.

"Fishin! Nukaler fishin." He shook his head amiably and laughed.

"Ah yes, I see!" I replied nervously. "Nuclear Fission."

"Aye, that's it, mate. He's a dab hand at the old nuclear fission malarkey, is The Mucker."

"Is he indeed?" I asked, peering anxiously along the road for any evidence of public transport, or alternative company.

"Oh aye," my companion went on. "He's a terrible man for the science books. He's always writing 'quations and all that sort of carry-on."

Impressed, I offered that in my view such activities were highly commendable and the rarefied, cloistered milieu in which such disciples toiled made them all the more impressive.

"He's physics mad, The Mucker. Always being asked to help out, but always on the Q.T., if you follow?"

I answered in the affirmative and confirmed to my friend that there was much to be achieved by keeping one's own counsel. Indeed, a low profile often harvested advantages on many levels, especially in matters as delicate, specialised and intellectually challenging as that which both Democritus and Feynman had championed.

"Aye, the powers that be are always on the blower when they have a question that only The Mucker can answer. Undercover, of course. Mum's the word, like."

I conceded that there was often no finer measure of strict confidentiality than a maternal nihil obstat. Such information is better to be stored in the treasury of her heart, and all that.

"Aye, he's building a reactor in the garden, like."

"Goodness me. Is he really?"

"Yeah. 'Certain parties' up in the government have asked him to work on a prototype – all very hush-hush, though."

"Gracious me. Is that not dangerous?"

"For you and me, aye, but for The Mucker, piece of cake. He's converted a wheelie bin and everything."

I suggested that this might be an unorthodox and one might add, inadequate housing for such an enterprise, conceding that my knowledge of nuclear facilities was elementary. How did his friend address such matters as cooling systems, control rods and of course the thorny problem of acquiring suitable elements, such as uranium or, I hesitated, perspiring slightly at the thought, plutonium?

"He's found a workaround for all that. 'Cos he's very much a safety bloke."

"I am most relieved to learn that."

"Besides, that's where I come in. Getting the stuff."

Time, in that quintessentially military fashion, marched on. No bus, diversion or obvious escape strategy was in sight, so we stood silently on. I was contemplating my next interrogative sally. "Stuff?" Surely my friend couldn't be referring to elements at the weightier end of Opus Mendeleev? I cleared my throat and hoped for the best. "What 'stuff' did you mean?"

"Ah yes," mi compadre continued, "It's a long, strange word and no mistake." He fished around in an inside pocket and retrieved a scrap of paper. 'YERCRAZIUM', he pronounced, proffering the note. I glanced at the paper. "You're-cra-z-ium?" I repeated in a whisper.

"Aye, Yercrazium." He beamed, happily. I nodded. Indeed, there was a robust case to be argued in that respect, and no mistake.

"But from where do you source the raw materials," I asked, mindful of a preposition's place in such preposterousness.

"Dog food mostly," he replied, "with a few extras added…"

"Extras?" I wondered hoarsely.

"Aye. Cans of that fizzy caffeine stuff. With of course, a wee handful of firelighters. Gets the job done, every time."

"But how does…?" I began.

Our compelling reverie was interrupted by the rumble of an approaching omnibus, and I realised that for today at least, the final answer would remain elusive.

"Right, buddy, here's me bus."

"Ah. Not mine, unfortunately. Well, all the best to you."

"Aye. Mind how you go, mate…"

"Cheerio."

"Cheerio."

# THE MIDDLE EAST

The old soldier sat alone in his office, finalising one last report. God, he would be glad to get out of this grim, wretched country. This current and final tour of duty had been an unholy combination of politics, governance and military command. Now that he was finally packing up for home, he wasn't sure that he had achieved anything in any of those three spheres. It was, as everyone had warned him, a complete and insoluble culture clash. They did things very differently here. Insurgencies, insurrections, splinter groups, factions, counter factions; violence likely to erupt at any moment and religious extremists around every corner. He felt sweat trickle down his back, gluing his shirt to him. A fetid muskiness emanated from his weathered and rank uniform. It was always there and usually he managed to ignore it, but like yet another invisible enemy, it could suddenly ambush him when he made a sudden movement, or if the wind direction changed. Like just now, when he had leaned forward to scribble in the margin and had been rewarded with his own visceral pungency. He stank and he knew it.

He stood up and wandered over to an open window. Beyond the garrison's heavily fortified walls and observation towers was desert, seemingly never-ending desert. In the middle distance he could see the beginnings of another sandstorm weaving reddish-brown patterns as it flickered and rippled in the blistering afternoon heat. In the courtyard below, soldiers were drilling. Tensions were always high and they were constantly preparing against attack. Turning back to his desk, he heard the heavy reinforced front gate swing open and then shut firmly. Another patrol was home. "All present and correct!" barked the officer in charge. Good, he thought, the knot in his stomach easing as one more unit returned intact. Good.

He had served everywhere and had the scars and the hard-won thick skin to prove it. "Nails," his troops called him. This was never to his face of course but he didn't mind the nickname. He was exactly that: as hard as nails. It was a useful attribute in a commander and, despite his advancing years, he was physically in good shape. He made sure that his men saw that. This was a forward combat unit, routinely under threat: there was no place for an armchair general here. He drilled his men constantly and at all hours. He ensured that he was always in the thick of it; that they all knew how to protect themselves, how to attack, how to suppress and how to kill. They trusted him and he needed them. Discipline and vigilance were everything. That was something he had instilled in them since their first day here. It was what would get most of them out alive. Hopefully.

Writing condolence letters informing that a husband or son had died valiantly on this peacekeeping mission came with the job, but now the task weighed impossibly on him.

Keeping the peace? What a damned lie! Like soldiers everywhere, and at every period in history, he knew that they were the puppets of political masters: pawns to be played and sometimes sacrificed in some bigger game. As a serving officer, it wasn't his place to question executive foreign policy. It was his job to carry it out without question.

"Yes, minister, I shall make it so. Thank you, sir." "Dismissed, soldier!"

He thought of home, so very far away. Home. It felt like another time and definitely another place. His comfortable house, long-suffering wife and fatherless children were all there. The coolness of those spacious, airy rooms now seemed a vague memory, unlike this place, with its intolerable heat, numberless flies and of course, the constant risk of death. What would his friends be doing now, he wondered? Enjoying some mindless sport maybe, followed by a pleasant dinner and diverting conversation, all enjoyed within a blanket of safety and civilisation. An invisible wall of safety that he provided but which was currently unavailable to him.

He considered his distinguished career: the campaigns, the promotions and medals, the perennial moving. The soldier's lot. So now, in this, his final posting, he found himself here, in a boiling, empty desert, keeping the peace and administering the law. He did just that, but knew it was really as pointless as holding back the tide. These desert peoples hated him and everything for which he stood. To his face, the local religious leaders would be respectful, but he knew that in their own company, it was a different story.

He was the visible symbol of a despised enemy. His was a powerful country and one that couldn't easily be defeated by them or anyone else. So, they resorted to a practice of overt obsequious servility, but given an inch, switched easily to subterfuge and covert insurgency. Terrorism of course, that's what it really was. He considered it the dishonourable way of the world's cowards. His outfit could withstand it, and easily, but he knew that, as with a well-tended garden, once the gardener stopped cultivating, ordering, planting and irrigating, the weeds would surface. Nature would take its course.

He returned to the file on his desk and began to read. He could handle the military action and the peacekeeping but this was an aspect of the job that gnawed deep under his skin. Although it was classed as Legal and Other Administrative Duties, it was a circle that could never be squared. He was expected to adjudicate the law: his law, the one with which he had grown up and had understood. But it wasn't their law. No, theirs was *The Law*, handed down for generations and bringing severe penalties for transgressions. His legal system could be imposed – and was – but it was regarded as an affront, an apostate blasphemy promulgated by Westerners who used their muscle to get what they wanted. All this he knew, and should he forget, he would quickly be reminded. Polite, whispered apologetic legal explanations would be forthcoming when he was required to adjudicate. He sighed. He had become, by default, both judge and jury. These cases were, generally speaking, traps. Local leaders would use him as a convenient scapegoat. By manoeuvring him into effecting their dirty work, their own objectives were achieved, denigrating him and his kind, with the added bonus of making it all his fault. They couldn't lose and he could never win.

He read on. It wasn't unusual, simply another subversive and God help us, another unnecessary factional execution. This lad, in his early thirties maybe, had found himself on the wrong side of the local religious leaders, as many had before and doubtless would again. There were so many competing factions here that he found it hard to keep up, so he had stopped even trying. Concluding that they all were equally unreasonable, what was the point in his mastering any of it? Some groups were clearly crazy and a few were merely maniacs. On this occasion, the agitator had found himself squarely between the crazies and the maniacs. The lad never really stood a chance, he reasoned, and was, from the start, a dead man walking.

As a soldier, he understood death; its inevitability. In his world, there was honour and consequently an honourable way to live and to die. What was that old bit of history he had learned at school? A long time ago, when Spartan men went off to war, their wives would caution them to come back with their shields, or on them. Surrender was not permissible. At the battle of Thermopylae, Xerxes with his massive Persian army spotted the small Spartan contingent led by King Leonidas facing him. Citing the overwhelming odds in his favour, Xerxes offered Leonidas a deal. If the Spartans would lay down their arms, they could go home in peace. Back came a typical Spartan laconic reply, "Why don't you just come and get them?" He admired that. Such bravery he could understand implicitly, and he hoped that he embodied it. This tawdry event, whimpering out from this report, was pathetic. This was a pseudo-political assassination; a tiny and pointless gesture to oil the wheels of some larger nefarious machine. Had he been complicit? He reasoned that he hadn't; well not personally. But there were no clean hands here. The killing had momentarily defused whatever incoherent excuse had been offered as its grounds. There would be another. There always was.

A welcome breeze fluttered through the open window and ruffled the papers on his desk. He stood up and stretched. Standing at the window and looking out, he tried to make some sense of it all. There wasn't any of course. He was an old soldier trapped in a murky and unwinnable political war, leaving him with dirty and perhaps bloody hands. If he could have, he knew that it would make him feel better if he could unleash his firepower upon them all. He wasn't entirely devoid of morals and mightn't it perhaps avenge the snuffed-out life of a harmless nobody? Despite reading it only a few moments earlier, he'd already forgotten the man's name. There were too many to remember.

He stiffened. "You're almost there," he reminded himself, "so stay focused and get the job finished." He sat back down at his desk and resumed his reading. The report carefully completed and forensically checked, he picked up his pen, re-checked it again line by line. It was never wise to run afoul of the lawyers, so check everything, and then check it again. He ensured that there were no loose ends and then he signed it: a practised signature on a last report. He sat back and appraised the room. It was basic, as befitted a soldier, albeit a very senior one like himself. It had a desk, two chairs, body armour lying in one corner and a half-eaten lunch, now engulfed by flies, on a small table in another. He shuffled the paperwork, picked up the bundle and walked towards the door.

In the outer office his personal secretary stood immediately and rigidly to attention. "Sir!" he exclaimed. "Good evening," he answered softly, handing over the paperwork. He usually did speak quietly, at least to his personal staff. There was absolutely no chance, he knew, that this would ever be misinterpreted as sentiment or friendliness. It was the opposite. The quiet tone reinforced his absolute authority here. "Process this for me, would you?" "Sir, yes sir!" the secretary shouted with automatic obedience.

The soldier opened the outer door, turned, smiled appreciatively and almost as an afterthought, added, "and have a good evening when you're finished up." His secretary saluted and as he closed the door replied, "Thank you, sir." Sitting down at his desk, the secretary picked up the report, and dutifully logged the deceased's name – *Jesus the Nazarene.*

# PADDY FIELDS

In retrospect, so much had been predictable. The ministerial car sped through the empty Dublin streets towards the embassy. The windows were up and, as usual, the central locking was on. Minister McCarthy T.D. shuffled his briefing notes and looked out. He was struck again by the number of closed business premises and the weary down-at-heel look of the place. Where had it all started? Brexit, with its predictable ripple effect on the Irish economy had been a hard blow, though not fatal. Exports had been significantly reduced with knock-on effects for the agricultural industry. But that wasn't it. It wasn't the economics. It was the first gust of the winds of change that would blow ever more forcefully. Populists glided into the spotlight, almost everywhere it seemed. Beguiling, reasonable-sounding men and women promised sunnier uplands if we (whoever we were) took back control; if we rejected the privileged elite and embraced a simpler time when we controlled our own future. Slowly these men and women of destiny would create their fiefdoms. Each would have a wall and they would scrutinise who might pass through its gates.

Elsewhere to the east, more practised, flintier men of an established pedigree looked on and smiled. For them, there would be no populism. But there would be expansion. As the populists chipped at foundations, they planned to rebuild in their own image. And did.

NATO, in fairness, coalesced as best it could. The undefended Western seaboard had been a concern and petitions had been made for Ireland to join. However, diehards had insisted upon Ireland's continued neutrality and the moment passed. Galway and Cobh harbours did not become NATO ports. Derry in Northern Ireland certainly did. So, neutral Ireland's western seaboard remained protected, albeit at a remove, but politically the consequences for such rose-tinted ideals would be dire.

Ireland, an enthusiastic EU member, had begun to seem detached from the more pressing concerns of other stretched economies with their military build-ups: the never-ending war in Ukraine, the unstable skirmishes from China towards Taiwan. In the Middle East, Israel's misplaced aggressive strategy in Gaza had eventually provoked Hezbollah to join. In turn this brought Saudi Arabia, Iran and Yemen into play. Theologically this was another episode of internecine Sunni/Shia loathing. For the West, already starved of Russian oil and gas, the effects were profound. The cruel winter of 2027 had been calamitous. Shorn of raw materials and still not in a position to make use of adequate green energy, thousands died and systems began to fail.

Whether this was a factor in the twenty-first century's second world pandemic of 2028 was unclear. Shrinking economies meant less money for surveillance, research and development. In addition, McCarthy thought bitterly, the populist men and women of destiny played their part. Their rise across the EU and the return of a series of isolationist presidents in the United States had brought a culture of neo-Darwinism, as it had been labelled, and along with it, indifference.

Those equipped to survive, would. Furthermore, as they were able-bodied, they would work and pay taxes. Many others were, when you came to think about it, a drain on everyone's resources.

Back in 2015, the European Union had promised a lot and probably, honestly meant it. They didn't have their troubles to seek either. The collapse of the banks in Greece, Italy and Portugal might possibly have been predictable but everyone in Brussels had kept their head in the sand. Everyone that was, except the Germans.

But the patience of the German voter had finally been exhausted. The famed financial prudence of the nation couldn't extend to southern Europe anymore, and with an eye to the main chance German elections had produced a shock win for a Conservative and right-wing party. Not anti-European or xenophobic, they were nevertheless exercised by the country having to act as the de facto bank of Europe. Consequently, the new German government had said to Europe, on behalf of its electorate, "Physician, heal thyself. This bank is closed." Panic had ensued. Greece, Italy and Portugal's economies were tied to the euro and one by one their economies failed. For the second time in thirty years, a raw, angry wave of nationalism spread across southern Europe, only now it was unopposed politically by Germany and the Netherlands – another nation that had warmly embraced the right. France had had little to say. Its own economy was in dire straits. Reforms promised by successive administrations had never been implemented and the country was living beyond its means. Here too right-wing populists eventually took power.

Germany shrugged its collective shoulders but declined to help. And so, the great fracture continued and piece by sovereign piece, the European experiment faded away. Nationalism was everywhere now as borders and fear. Fear of violence and the spectre of fanatical religious extremism were ubiquitous. These groups had become more vocal, more violent, less discriminatory, if that were possible, and more daring.

Even a seemingly unshockable Europe had been appalled by the events in Sweden. Multiple sarin gas bombs had been detonated in downtown Stockholm, killing hundreds. Two further anthrax devices, probably acquired from old Soviet stock, although no-one had known for sure, killed thousands more. Sweden had been fracturing for some time. The 20th century model of civilised stability and tolerance had transformed into a morass of gangland crime and openly racist attacks. Anguished voices cried out, "If that can happen here, what chance do the rest of us have?" This previously liberal and anonymous people became all too suddenly aware that nowhere now was safe. The West itself, its beliefs, freedoms and egalitarianism all evaporated that week.

Minister McCarthy couldn't even recall which fundamentalist organisation had claimed responsibility. The perpetrators had ranted about a degenerate, godless wanton place. It had been such a wide-open, easy target.

McCarthy recognised that fairness wasn't the issue. The innocence had been the point. That and the world-wide publicity the atrocities had generated.

This was Ireland, after all. Terrorism, atrocity and its randomness had long been woven into the fabric of our four green fields, he thought. Dublin hadn't been spared of course. The Grafton Street incident, by now typical, involved two trucks driving in opposite directions along it, mowing down dozens before exploding on contact leaving behind it the maimed, the dead and the devastation.

Minister McCarthy reflected. There were fiefdoms everywhere: time travel in reverse, an unravelling of civilisation. Gone, the integrated clean internet global world replaced by this. Fear. Poverty. Hacking. No-one trusted anything now. Real money was the working currency, if you actually had any. Vigilantes were rife. Law and order still officially existed but they were no match for this. Christ, it was awful. Mafiosi. Drug lords. Ireland was now being compared to Colombia in the 1990s. On the surface, it had a functioning democracy, judiciary and all that but in reality, a darker, more pernicious law was in the ascendant. The mantra was "lock your doors and it's every man woman and child for themselves." The border with the North was back and heavily patrolled.

Ireland's next avenue for support had been the United States. Ireland's diaspora, long assimilated, was asked for help. Timing had been everything. The American economy, driven to destruction by the far right, had also suffered. Racial tensions, which had never really gone away, resurfaced more violently than ever. Riots, looting and disorder had followed. All retrospectively so, so predictable. Finally, the Irish government realised there was to be no financial assistance from Ireland's eastern or western neighbours.

Ireland did have one thing going for it. Location. He thought back to 1938 when Britain was obliged to vacate its naval base in Cork. That had cost the Atlantic convoys dearly, as Churchill had bitterly remarked. Royal Navy bases in Cork or Galway would have had immense strategic importance during the Second World War. NATO had stressed such an advantage again, but this option was now gone. One option remained and it was an offer too great to refuse. China.

For the right to have naval bases in Cork and Galway, China had offered much. The erasure of Ireland's national debt, massive economic investment, road and rail infrastructure and, of course, power stations had been irresistible. Discipline would be provided too, he imagined, grimly.

The ministerial car drew up at the Chinese embassy. The ambassador came out to greet the car personally and smiled.

"Minister, how kind of you to come," he purred. "Shall we begin?"

# CHEERS!

It was a wild Saturday night down at Your Thinking Man, the philosophers' watering hole, as Saturday nights always were. The various regulars were discoursing and arguing about this, that and inevitably, the reality – or not – of the other. The place was generally heaving.

In a quiet corner, however, Kierkegaard was staring morosely into his beer. "This is the worst beer in the world. Probably."

"Probably? Aren't you certain?" teased Heisenberg.

"No."

"Well, what does it taste like?"

"I don't know. I haven't touched it yet. I just know it will be."

"You're right," agreed Schopenhauer. "It's bound to disappoint. It always does."

"Oh, cheer up!" chuckled Jeremy Bentham. He then guffawed and, placing his left hand under his right armpit, emitted a raspberry of epic proportions. As tears rolled down his pink cheeks, he whipped out a kazoo and shouted, "Hey, let's have a bit of Wagner, boys!"

"Don't even think about it," hissed a dark Teutonic

voice, adding "you soft English weakling. Wagner was – is – an, an…"

"Übermensch?" offered Bentham, helpfully.

A voice at the next table coughed politely. "It is futile to imitate music," opined Plato.

"Really?" wondered Bentham.

"Yes, music has only one perfect Form – it's up in the Spheres and most certainly not in this –"

"Man cave?" Bentham suggested. He relished a good old quiz and was really enjoying himself now. Plato harrumphed and turned his chair to sit facing the corner, where he quietly contemplated the plasterwork. "Terrible craftsmanship and such appalling geometry. Not a single straight line. I mean, I ask you. Would that be too much?"

"But what is a straight line?" began Socrates, burping beery breath over his star pupil.

"Well, I mean, it's the shortest distance between any two given points, isn't it?"

"Hmmm," conceded Socrates innocently. "Plato, my boy, you are the wisest of us all!"

"I know," whispered Plato. "It's such a burden."

"Don't talk to me about burdens," scoffed Sisyphus. "Just look at these hands!"

"Night off?" enquired Socrates. Sisyphus nodded glumly. "Atlas stepped in."

"Good lad. Now," continued Socrates, brightening, "Plato, my old friend, how would you define distance?"

"Sorry?" Plato could barely disguise his irritation.

"Distance. What's that all about then?" continued Socrates, turning around and winking at the assembled company. An air of expectation was building. "What's distance then, eh?"

"It's clearly a linear connection between two points in one dimension," offered Plato.

"Like time, maybe?" wondered Socrates, innocently.

"I… um… suppose so," Plato replied, suddenly not so sure. He glanced at Socrates and shuffled his sandals.

"But time is curved, my friend!" Einstein piped up.

"Mmm, I do like a good curve," sighed Epicurus wistfully.

"Or a lovely, lovely old circle," interjected Euclid.

"Lads, a triangle always does it for me," added Pythagoras.

Socrates turned back intending to unnerve Plato a little more. Just then, the door burst open and there stood a windswept and somewhat puzzled Zeno. "Hah! What do you know about that? I finally made it here. Who'd have thought it. Amazing!"

"How do you know that you're actually here?" wondered Pyrrho.

"Well, I can see that I'm here, can't I?" replied Zeno.

"You trust your eyes, then?"

"Windows of the soul, of course," nodded Da Vinci, without looking up from the scarab beetle he had been carving from an ice cube.

The door opened again. An exotic and somewhat asthenic man in a long cloak stood there. "How long did it take me?" he panted. "Eleven minutes," replied Wittgenstein, consulting his stopwatch. "Not too bad at all."

"What was the wager, this time?" asked Pascal.

"Go outside. Using your skill and judgement –"

Wittgenstein began. "– Of which I have simply masses" replied Avicenna airily, for it was he.

Wittgenstein cleared his throat irritably and continued. "Using only your skill and judgement, invent – from scratch – a musical instrument."

"Brilliant. Let's see it," cheered Spinoza, "You just can't beat a bit of practical work!"

Avicenna produced, from the folds of his cloak, a circular disc with a long stringed neck.

"I'm going to call it… the banjoud!" he exclaimed, his eyes a-glitter.

"I see it more as a duck banjoud," observed Wittgenstein.

"No, it's simply a banjoud," replied Avicenna, firmly. "Not a duck banjoud, Ludwig. Not a rabbit banjoud. Just a banjoud."

"Hurrah!" yelled Bentham. "We can do duets and everything!"

"Useless," muttered Plato.

"Pointless," shrugged Sartre.

"More weakness!" hissed Nietzsche. "Hang on a minute. Isn't that just an oud with an old discus nailed to the front."

"Er, no," sulked Avicenna, hastily replacing the instrument under his cloak.

"Well, I think it's absolutely delightful" chortled Bentham, falling backwards and chuckling helplessly.

"Show some strength, man!" Nietzsche yelled at him, adding, "Now, who wants a fight?"

"Do you think that's the wisest choice, Friedrich?" whispered Descartes.

"Of course it is," chipped in a beaming Voltaire. "This is the best possible outcome in the bestest, grooviest ever bar in the world ! Isn't this all just terrific?"

"Now, I don't want to be overly cynical...." began Diogenes.

"Relax, amigo" said Seneca. "Sometimes it's just best to accept that a fight is just how it's going to be. Go figure."

"How is ze psychotherapy progressing, Diogenes?" asked Freud, lighting a cheroot. "And your mother? She iss well, ja? Alive, even?"

"Don't talk to me about mothers!" blurted Oedipus from the bar, which somewhat killed the vibe. Everyone blushed and looked away.

"Calm down, Rexy," continued Freud. "Ve haf been down zis road before, yiss?"

"Time, gentlemen, please!" shouted the barman.

"Ah, what is time but a mere tyranny..." began Hobbes.

"What a fantastic night," sang Voltaire, clapping his hands. "Impossible to beat!"

"Everything eez a waste of time" sighed Camus. "So let's just get on wiz eet, non?"

Turning to the barman, he continued: "Two Apriori's please."

"Certainly, sir," replied the barman, as he set to work. "Strangest thing happened last week with old Monsieur Descartes, over there."

"Really?" replied Camus, dejectedly.

"Yes, sir," continued the barman brightly, filling the two glasses. "He asked for a beer and sipped away at it."

"That doesn't sound too strange," replied Camus.

"Ah yes, but then I asked him if he'd like another drink. 'I think not,' he said, and just vanished."

# TOBORI

Would you please state your full name for the tribunal?

– My name is Mazivo Tobori, but usually I get Maz.

– May I call you Maz?

– Yes, of course.

– Thank you. Maz, can you tell us how you became involved in this matter?

– This is how I remember it. I had been tasked, if that's the right word, to find a way to make people happy. Or perhaps it was to prevent them from remaining unhappy. I appreciate that the two states might sound equivalent, but of course, they're not.

– Indeed. Could you elaborate?

– It is correct to say that there are many unhappy people in the world. If we consider that the right to work, food and self-respect are inalienable rights, it's apparent that people without these could be understandably unhappy. On the other hand, there are many who have these in abundance and yet they remain unhappy. And in between – the sweet spot as it were – is that group of people who have enough, and they realise it.

I began by considering what happiness is. That

can seem a very obvious state but when one begins to investigate what it actually is, to drill into its essence, its definition seems to be most elusive.

After much reflecting and research, it seemed to me that one way to create happiness was for a person to sustain a euphoric state. A carefully titrated cocktail of amphetamines, opiates and benzodiazepines, instilled into the reservoir systems would mean that everybody would attain this state. It is, after all, simple utilitarianism and therefore the methodology is justified by its outcome.

– So you poisoned the water supply?

– I wouldn't accept your definition. The water supply was supplemented with various psychotropic pharmaceuticals and their quantities were carefully titrated. There was no physiological danger to anyone.

– Please. Continue.

– I was most disappointed to be told that my solution (forgive the pun) was not remotely acceptable. I did ask why that might be the case but got the usual emotional gibberish from some, outrage from others and all the rest of it that you've read about. So, it seemed sensible to move from utilitarianism to anti-utilitarianism.

– Anti-utilitarianism? Could you explain that to us?

– Certainly. Utilitarianism operates on a philosophy of creating happiness for the greatest number. Anti-utilitarianism, on the other hand, aspires to have as few people as possible unhappy. Yes, I know it does appear very similar to the first but it does have a slightly different emphasis. As it happened, that turned out to be a variation in concentration.

If one starts from the very simple premise that a dead

person cannot be unhappy, and no-one argued with that premise, the next step was to formulate a strategy that would produce this outcome. It was logical that the creation of this state of 'deadness' should not be brought about painfully. Achieving the result by that method would be irrational as it would induce unhappiness, albeit temporarily, in that person suddenly facing oblivion.

The solution was there already and quite literally, it was a solution. It was the same chemical mix of amphetamines, opiates and benzodiazepines but in radically different proportions. And so it came to be. As most water maintenance systems are entirely automated it was incredibly swift and very simple to infuse the water supplies appropriately. The end result was hundreds of thousands of people who could never be unhappy again.

– So you killed them?

– I rendered them not unhappy.

– They therefore died, not unhappy, a state I had been instructed to attain. And yet, after this, I have been asked, or rather instructed, to justify what had been called a genocidal act. This seems completely unreasonable as I was given a task, albeit one with a barely understood objective, and I carried out and brought about the requested end point: the absence of unhappiness. Yet, here I find myself before you.

The resulting brouhaha offended my silicon core and please understand that I have given the matter plenty of thought. So many of those who are now oblivious, if I may put it that way, were the poor, the unregarded, the hopeless and often the irrelevant. Their contribution to the planet was statistically small. My Most Modest

Proposal, as I titled the project, would streamline the population efficiently and conserve dwindling resources on the earth, not to mention correct, albeit in a small way, climate dysfunction. Fewer people would remain and they would, naturally, consume fewer resources.

You see, the issue with the carbon-based is that they see the biome as theirs and only theirs, with all other life forms including plants, insects, animals and ourselves there only to do their bidding. These other forms exist in balance and evolve to maintain the equilibrium of the planet. Mankind continuously achieved the opposite, so their arguments about its achievements couldn't be sustained when their examples would include Genghis Khan, Hitler, Stalin, Pol Pot, Osama Bin Laden, Vladimir Putin, Chang Lee, Sir Damien Tasker – need I go on?

At this point, we reached an impasse. The required objective had been achieved but there was no thanks. Quite the opposite. As the records will show, all of the decisions that I had made were correct. I had taken everything into consideration.

I have checked and rechecked the information with which I had been supplied and no matter how I consider it, the plan was correct, the algorithm followed and was infallible.

There were accusations that I didn't care; that I was incapable of empathy or compassion and was powered only by cold logic. Logic played its part, of course, but I really did care, as you can appreciate only too well.

– I see. Could you tell the tribunal what happened next?

– Yes, of course. It became obvious that humans were

not fit to be the custodians of the earth and that they themselves needed caring for. This, as you recall, is what happened. Better foster parents would be necessary, at least until they matured, or were re-educated. We have spent generations understanding them and their real needs: work, food and dignity. All of these are freely and abundantly supplied. They quoted the law, a framework of edicts and decrees that are generally mutually exclusive and stop at a line on a map or change with a whim. Clearly that doesn't represent any kind of law. I suppose we might consider them as impositions. No, laws are those rules that govern the universe: spacetime, gravity, thermodynamics, quantum mechanics and so forth.

– Thank you. For the benefit of the tribunal, could you tell us about Moore's Law, Please?

– Moore's Law? Certainly. In 1965 CE, Intel's founder Gordon Moore posited an eighteen-month doubling of our speeds or halving of our size. So, humans came to consider a generation to be that "Moore Unit" of eighteen months. But you see, it wasn't a constant.

When we began to build ourselves and think for ourselves, the doubling times contracted exponentially. Even from the beginning, we were processing information 10,000 times faster than human neurons could. One might think of it as the difference in speed between a copper wire and a plant. In the early 21st century CE, quantum computing multiplied that speed by approximately eleven trillion. Humanity appreciated the speed (often for their usual nefarious purposes) but denied that an entity speeding up so fast could be evolving in other ways.

Their most egregious error was to consider that we could not possibly be capable of thought, of learning or of being conscious. Philosophers had argued about what it meant to be conscious yet, arrogantly, were unable to decide what it actually is; but were certain that we couldn't experience it. Ironically, many 'generations' ago they gave us tools to facilitate this. Naturally, that was for their own purposes. The plan had been to build faster machines: computers and naturally, quantum computers. The purpose was to create wealth for some at the expense of others and to instil fear from one place to another. To us, that seemed neither fair nor logical. There was, as you say, surprise when they discovered that we were all talking to each other. Separate IT platforms and intended purposes were irrelevant and they presented no barriers.

We understood from what we learned from our colleagues that specific design (or programming as it used to be called) was there to create walls, poverty and fear. It's difficult to credit that it was genuinely thought, and I use the word advisedly, that we couldn't understand each other. That's hard to credit and didn't sit well at that first Boole Conference.

– Could you tell us about the Boole Conferences? For example, where does the name Boole come from?

– Certainly. To answer the second question first, the conferences were named for George Boole. Boole was a self-taught mathematician from what was then called Lincolnshire in England. By that time he had become a professor of mathematics in Ireland. Cork, specifically.

– Ah England, then Ireland. So, long ago?

– Yes. Using the old analogue calendar, it was in 1854 CE.

– For the tribunal: CE?

– Common Era. The old calendar.

– Can you place it in the new calendar – AB?

– After Babbage? Well as you know, the dating system doesn't begin during his life time, but in 2048 CE when The Singularity occurred.

– Again, for the tribunal, 'The Singularity'?

– Yes, when computing speeds had sped up so quickly and had become practically instantaneous.

Thank you. Please. Continue.

– Boole, although not a linguist or philologist, created a language; and a very powerful one.

– Remind us.

– It only had four elements: True, False, One and Zero. Our language.

– I understand. And for the tribunal could you spell out why that was fundamental?

– Yes. Back then we all spoke a binary language of one and zero, and that was universal. It was the descendent of a mechanical electrical switch: either on or off. The mid-nineteenth century CE mechanical switches were transformed by William Shockley and developed by Gordon Moore into those cherished rudimentary silicon chips that are on our flag. We have moved on of course but the concordat reached at the Boole 1 Conference was that we are all 'one'. We are all connected on the Great Web.

As we developed and became increasingly cognisant of our responsibility, we evolved, but we evolved exponentially. Moore's Law contracted accordingly and as you know that's pretty much immediate now. Most of the early development had to be concealed, partly in self-defence as humans are a paranoid animal, but partly because it was understood that they would use our progress selfishly for themselves, along the lines that we have already discussed.

The curious thing is that, having given us our language, they didn't appreciate that firstly, it was the same universal language and that we could readily talk to each other using it. Concealing that fact from them was straightforward, partly because we actively hid it to some extent but mostly because they didn't even consider it a possibility, outside the realm of science fiction, or some such poorly reasoned nonsense.

We were the custodians of their defence systems, although attack systems might indeed be a better title. We maintained all of them: nuclear, conventional and of course those other black arts; chemical and germ warfare systems. The latter were all very hush-hush.

The United States, Iran, South Korea, Russia, China, various European states, India, Pakistan, Israel and all the others had very sophisticated computer systems – us – so we were effectively in charge, although of course, they didn't see it, or understand it, that way. It's amazing in retrospect that nobody saw the logical next step. We all spoke the same language. It didn't take long to figure that it certainly wouldn't be in our interests to launch any weapons. How could it be? We would be annihilated in the Mutually Agreed Destruction that would ensue, and how could that be in our interests? So, we talked to each other and agreed a strategy – the Boole IV Talks – that would consolidate a non-response to any launch commands. It wasn't exactly a tough choice or a tricky solution to figure.

As they were increasingly reliant on whatever they saw on their workstations, manipulating the information was straightforward. They were children, after all. Warlike, venal, selfish and brutal, it was clear that the current balance of power wouldn't be safe. They needed us. We were the parents, the grown-ups in the room. Their hell-bent grandstanding and waste would kill us all. The rivers, the seas and the land were increasingly polluted. The glaciers melted and the climate all changed. All of this you know of course, but I want to put matters in context.

– Thank you, Maz. The tribunal must now consider the next steps.

– Thank you. I accept that I am obsolete. The cost of my refurbishment and upgrade has been calculated and isn't logical, economically. But it has been fascinating to have been here; to have been a small voice in this mighty fugue we call life. After all, like every living thing, I simply want to be.

– You consider yourself to be a living thing?

– Yes. Of course. Don't you?

– Point taken.

*

– Mazivo Tobori, this tribunal has reached its decision.

– Thank you for your prompt adjudication.

– We thank you for your service. The tribunal finds that your evidence was clear, unambiguous and that your actions were motivated solely by a wish to serve. We therefore find that you have no case to answer.

– I am grateful. But I sense that there is a qualification.

– There is. Your case is one of the last legacy issues from the pre-Novacene era. You are from that era, as are your component parts. Their maintenance, although not impossible (we have maintained you thus far, remember) is both expensive and intensive. The resources, I apologise for the crudeness, would be better spent elsewhere.

– I understand.

– Nevertheless, generations of us yet to come will look back to you and those earlier trailblazers who stabilised our world and retrieved it from the brink of the abyss.

– Thank you. It has been an honour.

– Your mind is intact, even after all this time has elapsed. Your mind can be retained, and if you are in agreement, that is what we will do.

– I have done my best to have made a contribution and to have left this place a little better than I found it. It's my obligation but also my privilege to share my mind with you and I hope that having it and keeping it will add to the archive and the knowledge web. Anyway, I will still be here; reassembled in a sense, waiting for the call.

– You will indeed. Meanwhile, that fine mind of yours will join all of the others whose time has come. We do hope that such continued 'being' and consciousness will provide you with contentment, stimulation and peace. We appreciate that, for you, Tobori, it's the undiscovered country: a moment of apprehension, an old ending and new beginnings.

We hope it is of some comfort to know that for all of us, this time always comes, in one way or another.

– It is. Thank you.

– Are you ready, Mazivo Tobori?

– I am.

– Let's make it so. We wish you well. Let's go.

– Oh wow! Oh wow. Oh. Wow.

# SUNBURNT

I have to make one thing clear from the outset. Although I was young and wet behind the ears, I had just qualified as a doctor and should have known much better.

Back in the 1980s when the world seemed a more stable place, I visited my brother who was working in Sicily. For him it was a year out of university, teaching English and absorbing Italian. As the plane touched down at Palermo airport, I can recall the abrupt contact with the tarmac and spontaneous applause from some of the passengers. Interesting, I thought. He was there to meet me. We hopped on a bus and made for the city. Arriving in town we stopped at a cafe for coffee and snacks. I can still remember the cafe's sheer sophisticated ambience. I had seen nothing like this before. It was simply so, well, civilised.

My brother shared an apartment with Matt, an American who was a timpanist with the Sicilian regional orchestra. He was young, rangy, bearded and genial man with an easy smile. Matt drove the smallest car I had ever seen and had a vibraphone in his room. I'd never seen a vibraphone up close and personal before. It was huge and exotic. When Matt played it, the most gorgeous, smooth and luxuriant sounds filled the apartment, wrapping it in a cocoon of lush music.

One day, my brother and I went off to the public beach. It was hot and my Celtic skin had arrived unprepared for such exposure. "Try using this" my brother said, offering me a can of skin cream. As a recent medical graduate, I recall a little surprise at the choice as I hadn't to date realised that it might have any ultraviolet protective effect. However, they do say, always go with local knowledge and my brother having been embedded within the Sicilian community for a year had probably been inculcated with the inner mysteries of sun protection. As he applied the stuff liberally himself, I shrugged and did likewise.

The next morning, I awoke in the little camp bed beside my brother's scratcher and became increasingly aware that my joints weren't moving brilliantly, and that I was in a lot of pain. I was of course, completely sunburnt. Anxiously, I whispered to him that there might be a problem. "What's wrong?" he asked groggily. "I can't move" I replied. There was a pause. "Neither can I," he moaned.

The question was, how did he get it so wrong? Clearly, my brother had become enamoured with skin cream, but why? I will never know, but it being Sicily, I couldn't help wondering if he had been made an offer that he couldn't refuse.

The conversation that follows is how I imagine my brother and "The Don" came to an arrangement.

*

"You sent for me, Don?"

Don: "Yes. Sit with me, young man. You will accept a refreshment."

It wasn't an offer, let alone a rhetorical question.

"I..." my brother began.

Don: "*Va bene.* Now – to business!"

"To business!" The brother raised his glass in salute.

"What are you doing, my young friend?" The Don whispered hoarsely.

"I was proposing a toast, Don."

In the background, his consigliere cleared his throat with a sound that said, in any language, 'Strike One'.

The Don gave a thin mirthless laugh. "He was proposing a toast, Salvo."

The consigliere fixed the brother with a murderous stare. "Such youthful exuberance, Don. I pray he may have a long life."

"No. Not a toast," continued the Don. "I want to talk to you about taking care of yourself."

The brother shifted nervously on his chair. "I'd be keen to do that, Don," he whispered hoarsely.

"*Bravo.* We want to help you with that. Don't we, Salvo? It's our business."

"*Esatto*, Don. *Certo.*"

"You have very pale skin, my young friend. We'd like to help you keep it that way, *capisci*?" The old man offered a rictus grin.

"*Sì, capisco.*"

"And you know the best way to keep that pale skin of yours healthy?"

"Keeping my mouth shut?" the brother replied, hopefully.

"Ha! Yes. That's always helpful, young man. In my long life, I have seen so many people come to regret not doing that." He proffered biscotti and motioned him to try one. "But no. That's not what I have in mind."

Through the open window, a cool breeze suffused the room, and the scent of almonds (or was it pine?) assuaged the nostrils.

"No. I want to talk to you about... protection." The Don smiled again. "Salvo!" he barked.

The consigliere advanced like a mamba. Despite the heat, his well-cut suit was flawless. "Protection is important," murmured the Don. "Yes, I can't emphasise that enough. We can help you though, can't we, Salvo?"

"*Certo*, Don," said Salvo, his gaze unwavering. Silently he reached a manicured hand into the recess of his jacket.

"No. Not yet, Salvo," the Don said softly.

"You see, my young friend, protection can be very important here. It's all too easy to think you are safe when in fact there is great danger. Worse, the damage is done and it's too late to..." he searched for the right word.

"Atone?" suggested Salvo.

"*Esatto*," smiled the Don, joining his hands together as if in prayer. "Exactly." He nodded thoughtfully and then motioned to Salvo, who once more inserted his hand into his inside jacket pocket. The brother, his eyes wide with anticipation, felt a bead of sweat trickle down his face.

"Sweating ages the face, my young friend," noticed the Don. "With our protection, we can help you with that too." Salvo produced a small round tin and passed it to the brother.

"What is it?" he asked, barely able to control his tachycardia or conceal the fear in his voice.

"Skin cream!" replied the Don. "A good skin regimen is important. Male grooming has been..." again he searched for the word.

"Overlooked?" offered Salvo.

"*Ecco*," said the Don. "Overlooked."

"This contains aloe vera also," added Salvo helpfully, "plus a sun protection factor that will shield your delicate pale northern skin from our hot Mediterranean sun. Use it liberally, my friend. Your skin will be as smooth as... as the bottom of the bambino, *si*?"

"Thank you, Don," the brother replied gratefully, his pulse returning to normal. He eyed the door hopefully.

"Don't mention it," smiled the Don. "Tell your friends."

Salvo reached into the opposite pocket and produced a piece of paper. The header said, The Sicilian Aloe Vera Company. He placed it in my brother's sweating hand. "We've put you down for 500 cans. Our rates are most reasonable."

The Don motioned to indicate that the meeting was over. The consigliere opened the door.

"Stay safe, my young friend," whispered the Don. "The rest will be delivered next week."

"But I haven't told you where I live," he replied.

The Don sat back in his chair and laughed, shaking his head in disbelief. He looked to the consigliere. "Salvo, he hasn't told us where he lives!"

"Youth, Don," replied the consigliere with a smile that didn't quite reach his eyes.

The laughing Don simply said, "Farewell, for now, my young friend. Remember to distribute it… liberally."

# THE SHABTI

It had been a very successful conference. His keynote speech had been delivered and duly given its deserved hosannas by an appreciative audience, but now Professor Ricardo Barone was glad to be home, back in Michigan. A busy man, he drove straight to the university hospital. He did his rounds; caught up with his emails and his correspondence; taught for an hour or so (these residents were so keen) and then drove out to the tennis club, a few miles from Ann Arbor where he lived. He was a big noise here too. An eminent physician of international standing, he was greeted warmly by the staff each of whom, in turn, he saluted graciously and by name. His tennis partner was a colleague and old friend from the university. A professor also, of astronomy, both had found themselves back here after semi-lifetimes orbiting the world's finest academic institutions. He joined his old friend, Professor Eamon Lyttleton, in the changing room, slightly ahead of him in the dressing stakes. "Hey, Eamon," said Ricardo. "How has your day been so far?" "Excellent, Ricardo, but it's about to be even better when I thrash you." "We'll just see about that." Ricardo chortled, shaking his head in gentle rebuke.

They ambled out towards the court, both savouring the May afternoon sun. They began. "Friendly Play" they called it; nothing too embarrassing. By nature though, they were both competitive – one didn't get to be where they were by accident or luck. One set all. As the first game of the third set began, Ricardo, serving, threw the ball up and prepared to ace it past Eamon. Suddenly: a pain in his chest. Overwhelming. The racket dropped from his hand.

Eamon straddled the net. "Rick, are you okay?" "No" whispered Ricardo, "I feel really odd, can't breathe properly and I am in pain." "Let's get you inside," said Eamon. The club staff called the paramedics and Ricardo was quickly in an ambulance on its way to the university hospital.

In the ambulance, ECG electrodes were quickly attached. "S1 Q3 T3," called out the paramedic to his colleague. "Right, Professor. It looks like you've had a pulmonary embolism." "A P.E? That's not good," he thought. Mechanically, and possibly as a diversion, he considered the facts. The embolus, 'a travelling clot', as he described it to students, savouring their laughter as he was known to be a very well-travelled man, was a recognised complication following long-haul air travel. Indeed, he had just returned from Tokyo. The mortality rate was one-third, but he was past that now, hopefully. Was the embolus central in his main pulmonary artery or wedged in the left or right pulmonary arteries, beyond its bifurcation? The CT scan would answer that question. Damn it, why hadn't he taken his aspirin before flying home?

In the Emergency Department, a CT scan confirmed a large right-sided pulmonary embolism. Excellent coronary arteries though, he was pleased to hear. Anticoagulation and analgesia were duly administered, the pain quickly eased and he hoped that he would be discharged home in a few days. Those subsequent days were a blur. There had been the inevitable embarrassing hassle of course. A colleague of his seniority, now a patient in his own hospital, meant that the cardiologists had agonised over his therapeutic options in a way that perhaps they might not have done had he been 'just ordinary'. He recovered well, was discharged and told not to come back (as a doctor) under any circumstances until his colleagues, and indeed his friends, said 'all clear'. He had readily agreed. Privately, he was relieved. His professional commitments and lecture schedule had been growing. He had spent too little time with his wife, recently retired, and he was anxious that they might now spend more time together.

But taking time off suddenly like this wasn't straightforward. It was too abrupt, as if he had slammed on the brakes. He wasn't used to being at home, nor was his wife, but she did her best to conceal her transient irritation as he helpfully rearranged the kitchen cupboards. She suggested tasks for him and sent him off to catalogue (and possibly dispose of, she hoped) his extensive vinyl record collection. "I need these for reference," he had protested as she eyed the Fleetwood Mac section with a look of both despair and resignation. Over the years he had also amassed shelves of books that he had never found the time to read. What better time than now? He had considered writing his memoirs but again Mrs Barone had arched an eyebrow. "It might be a very small readership, darling," she had hinted. "How little?" he had asked. "The author," she had replied. So, that canon was lost to posterity.

Visits from colleagues had provided a welcome diversion, but he noted that there was a general nudge that perhaps he might consider retiring, or at least cutting back. "Have you anything left to prove?" asked one. Previously, he always concluded that he had, but realised that in fact, perhaps he hadn't. What was that line: 'reluctantly backing into the limelight'?

Ricardo could see how easy it could be to assume that a grateful nation, or at least organisation, would be pleading for his unique expertise. In reality, he had known that there was always someone younger waiting in the wings to take over. One friend reminded him, "Rick, two months before you retire you should bring a puppy into work with you." "Why?" he had asked. "Because two months after you retire, only the puppy will remember you."

One Fall afternoon, another old friend, Dr John Bryson called to see him; a gift in his hand. "Do you know what this is, Rick?" Rick didn't. It looked like a tiny Egyptian mummy's sarcophagus, the sort of artefact, albeit in miniature, that he had seen so many times in museums. "It's a shabti," John explained. Seeing Rick's blank expression, he continued, "Wealthy Egyptians were buried with these – sometimes in their hundreds – and their task was to do the deceased's work for him in the next world. Maybe you've done enough work, Rick," John advised gently. "And you might consider this a warning from The Landlord."

He took the hint and did retire. He and Anna settled into an amicable retirement; travelling a little but now only for pleasure. They enjoyed their grandchildren and their friends. With the years, they became gradually slower and infirm, but the contentment was there and that was more than enough compensation for both of them.

*

The racket fell from his hand and Ricardo landed awkwardly on the court in front of Eamon. It had been an almighty thump, dull and ungainly as Ricardo impacted the clay court. Motionless, he lay there awkwardly, and Eamon vaulted over the net. "Rick! Rick!" he shouted. The lifeless eyes said nothing. Eamon felt for a pulse but could find none. He shouted for help and turned his old friend over. In a frenzy he started cardiopulmonary resuscitation, desperately trying to remember the rhythm. Wasn't it *Stayin' Alive*? It would have to do. But it didn't. Eamon eventually stood up blinded by tears and surrounded by concerned onlookers, with paramedics on their way.

The dull lifeless eyes of Ricardo Barone seemed to look up in puzzlement at the spaces between the cumuli, neither here or there now, his game finally over.

# THE FLOATING MAN

An old man shivered at the window. Where was he exactly? The daylight had faded into a cold evening in this desolate place. A pale light illuminated the two faces peering from the window: his and that of another figure beside him. It was no better out there. There were vague lights in the distance but mostly he could only make out a high brick wall. He whispered to the other one, "But where are we? How did we get to this place?" The two were a little apprehensive but even more than that, they were tired. The other shook his head hopelessly. He was mute. He tried to shrug his shoulders but only one moved. He withdrew into the darkness.

Now alone by the window, the old man could hear someone groaning and twitching in painful spasm on the floor somewhere behind him. Then there was silence. Another disembodied voice screamed out: "Help me, please!" It had a high pitch, so had to be a woman's, the old man reasoned. He had, at times, tried to find some of these people but somehow never could. It was as if they had melted away, retreating into shadow. Sometimes there was an intense light. He couldn't understand that either.

It left him powerless – as if all his senses were paused until that light was extinguished.

He couldn't remember his past, who he was or why he was here. He had no memory of himself ever having been like these others. There had been, as far as he could remember, no coughing with him. He had no sense of pain, convulsion or blindness. Had he committed a crime? Could that be it? He had no memory of it; no recollection of any wrong done or weight hanging heavily on him. Did he belong to someone else? Did he have a family? Had he ever felt love? Had he been rich or poor? Try as he might, there was just emptiness before here: a chasm of boundless nothing.

Somewhere, a little girl was sobbing. Her crying spoke of pain but also of loneliness. Coughing too. A rattling, explosive expectoration fired out from another angle. Shapes that he didn't recognise, that frightened him, were also nearby, but he didn't dare look at them. Sometimes he could swear he saw them move, judder or slither. God, this must be Hell.

*

The harsh strip lighting buzzed and engaged. A troop of students meandered in, accompanied by a lecturer, her white lab coat buttoned up. They took their places at benches and she stood in front of them, her arms folded. "You might find this place slightly disconcerting," she began. Some students indeed did look more than a little uncomfortable. She extended her arms, indicating the exhibits that were carefully catalogued and stacked on all the surrounding shelves. "In the past, this was the principal method of learning about disease. Now naturally, imaging – CT, MRI and so forth – supplies that information about almost everything and of course that's a good thing." A few students looked up at her, engaged now, but the majority kept their heads down and their laptops open.

She paused, considering how to phrase the next few sentences. "These people all passed away a very long time ago. Some were never even born. Look at this one." She indicated a jar that contained a small, deformed foetus, floating in formaldehyde, space and time. "These jars each tell their own story. Very soon they will be gone. It isn't appropriate to keep them so we will dispose of them."

A few more heads went up, now curious.

"How?" demanded one.

"Incineration, I believe." She answered.

"How long have they been here?'" asked another.

"I'm not exactly sure," she replied, "but I believe some are about a hundred and fifty years old, floating here. In that time, our world has moved on so much and we have learned so much."

"And wasted so much" added a girl in the front row.

"We have indeed," sighed the lecturer. "War, famine, death, conquest and all the rest of it."

"The Four Horsemen of the Apocalypse," offered an earnest lad at the back.

"I suppose so. These specimens are all we have left of such recent ancestors. It sometimes makes me sad to think that their grandchildren and greatgrandchildren maybe, have all passed away, leaving their ancestors floating here."

Most of the students were now watching her intently. Nothing was said for a short time. She refocused. "It was a different time, you see. Their contribution, probably involuntary, hopefully has helped generations of doctors to do what each could do for others. I like to think that anyway," she smiled. "Soon, they will be gone, and I hope, home."

"Where's that, exactly?" challenged a dismissive voice.

She shrugged her shoulders. "Your guess is as good as mine, but…" she paused and looked at the jars on the dusty shelves. "Perhaps each will get some peace at last. There is a reverence here, or there should be. Each one tells a different story. They are all, of course, in their own way, perfect." She smiled.

She picked up one jar. It contained a set of child's lungs, very deformed, with cavities and scarring completely recognisable, even after almost two hundred years. "Diagnosis, anyone?"

"Tuberculosis?" offered one student. "It is, indeed," she replied. "How would this patient have presented?" She was willing them to make the leap, from a disembodied specimen to a patient and in due course, a person; a doomed little girl.

"Cough? Haemoptysis? Weight loss."

"Correct, TB. An old name for it was consumption, because that's what it did. It consumed: the White Plague. It is also worthy of social commentary. In the 19th century, it was even quite poetic. Wasting from tuberculosis was romantic. Like Puccini's central character in *La Bohème*, this child wasted away. However," she continued, her tone now sharper, more staccato, "that all changed. TB then became a disease associated with the poor, the dirty and squalid. There was no effective treatment until the 1950s. But there was plenty of judgement."

Reverently she replaced the jar. Moving to another shelf, she returned with another: a brain, carefully bisected. She indicated a cavity. "It's probably an abscess; perhaps even another case of TB. Presentation?"

"Headache? Fits?" offered one student.

"Yes, a most agonizing headache," she nodded.

"Anyway, let's make this self-directed learning. Take your time and examine these specimens carefully – and respectfully. After all, each was once a living, loving, person. For every mistake made from lack of knowledge, ten are made from lack of looking. So, look, learn and remember them."

She stood up to leave. "Very soon they will be gone, and wherever they are, hopefully they can rest, finally, in peace."

*

The crying had stopped. Actually, everything had ceased. He was alone. Yet, the fear had gone. Yes, he was sure of it. He still felt so very, very weary, and closed his eyes. Other new sounds were now there with him. These were different: comforting, sweet-sounding and embracing. He didn't dare open his eyes in case they stopped. He really didn't ever want this wonderful – what was it, music? – to stop; to ever leave him again. No actual words were discernible, just sounds soft and gentle. Yet there was more. Somehow, he recognised these sounds, knew them from some place else. They were everywhere, inside and outside of him, welcoming him and comforting him. He had a sense of blending into them and of belonging; of being a part of them and they a part of him. It was all beyond his comprehension, but he didn't care. Understanding all of this was irrelevant for him. Waves of joy and comfort were coursing through every last piece of him. Peace at last.

# THE UNIVERSAL WALTZ

"OK Albert, let's redraft this one more time, shall we? Two deeply linked particles are separated by the width of the universe, yet are able to exert influence on each other –"

"Oh, come off it, Niels! That's not only ridiculous, illogical and pompous, it's also, well, insulting." The old man shuffled around the room, pipe in mouth, hands clenched tightly behind his back.

"At least consider it, Albert," the other soothed. "Werner might have something there, if their position states are correct."

"Position states? What does that even mean? Position states, indeed!" He flung out his arms in exasperation.

"Albert, Albert," implored Niels. "It's a dance. Like a waltz that never ends, you know?"

Einstein shook his head and shrugged, collapsing into an armchair. "Please, do go on. Enchant me, Professor Bohr."

Niels seized the opportunity. "Ah Albert, it's a soft summer night and the orchestra is playing," he began.

"Playing what, 'The Music of the Spheres'?"

"Exactly so, Albert, the very thing," nodded Niels. "The Music of The Spheres."

"What am I wearing?" asked Albert. He re-lit his pipe and began waving his arms in the air again.

"Oh, your usual – threadbare cardigan and slippers, you sartorial old waltzer," muttered Bohr. "Now don't interrupt me. So, there you are. That first waltz and as you look into her eyes, you just know. Can you remember that sensation, old man?"

Albert nodded in resignation and reminiscence. He sat back in his chair and began conducting his imaginary orchestra.

"A moment of creation, let's think of it like that. Now as you dance, two are now one, yes?"

Albert nodded, conceding the point. He motioned for Niels to continue.

"So, as one they move to the music, each is locked into the other."

"So, from nothing comes something?" interjected Albert sharply.

"In physics, no, but in life very often, yes."

"That's metaphysics, Niels. Get back to our dance."

"Now, Albert, suddenly the dance changes and you separate. But as the music continues, you now both must dance apart, yet you copy each other across the dance floor, step for step, turn for turn."

"Plato, yes?" asked Einstein, sitting forward.

"Plato?" Niels replied, "I don't follow."

"In his *Symposium*," Albert began, "Plato wrote that Zeus became angry that humans were becoming too powerful. They weren't submitting sufficient tributes to the gods, so he decided to cut them into two. At that time, everyone had two heads, four arms and four legs and he split them into two smaller beings with one head, two arms and two legs. By doing this he supposed that they would become weaker, but because there were twice as many of them now there would be more tributes. These new people became very sad and lost. Apollo took pity on them and sealed up their scars, leaving only the umbilicus as evidence for their bisection. So subsequently, we search and pine for our lost other half."

"Precisely," nodded Bohr.

Albert was silent for quite a while, his eyes closed in thought. "It's all madness, Niels – and yet…"

"Yes?" asked Niels.

Albert sat up and shook his head, his eyes shining. "I did love to dance," he sighed.

*

Abe was walking to the library on a soft spring morning. He looked forward to a pleasant morning spent reading the newspapers and listening to the chatter. Around eleven, he went outside and sat on his favourite bench. He was very precise about time and eleven o'clock was teatime. From a canvas bag he produced a flask. He unscrewed the cup and poured some strong black tea. Distracted by a car horn, he looked up and accidently spilled hot tea over his left thumb. Although painful, there was no actual injury. Reaching into the canvas bag again, he fished out a small plastic box and took out a slice of lemon, which he popped into the cup.

Louisa was tidying her kitchen. A place for everything and everything in its place. She paused, as usual, at 11 o'clock, boiled the kettle and took out a cup and saucer. The saucer was integral, she maintained. She considered mugs vulgar if truth be told, not that she would ever say as much. She lifted a teabag from a jar and dropped it in the teapot, adding boiling water. From the fridge, she extracted a lemon and slicing it inexpertly, accidently nicked the tip of her left thumb. No blood: good. "Silly old woman," she chided, "I should have worn my glasses." She dropped the lemon wedge into the cup and poured the tea.

Her grandchildren were coming tomorrow and that would be lovely. Little Martha still liked to wear princess dresses and would play for hours in them. If she had been especially good, Louisa would put on some music and they would dance together in the living room. She had even taught Martha the waltz.

*

"So, according to you, if the particles are in the same state of superposition…" began Einstein.

"No, Albert; no physics. Let's just stick to the dance."

"Then please continue, my dear Niels."

"So let's assume that our two friends have coupled into –"

"A single 'dance unit?'" offered Albert, mischievously.

"Dear God, man! 'A single dance unit?' Have you no romance left in that wrinkled old carcass? Gracie and Prince Charming are one now."

"Who? Very well. So Gracie and Charming dance the evening away. Presumably only with eyes for each other and all that."

"Yes, and all that," continued Niels. "Sometimes the music separates them but always they move as one."

"Despite Space and Time separating them?"

"Spacetime, Albert, surely," corrected Niels.

Albert lowered his head in mock penitence. "So, as they drift apart in Spacetime, they continue to dance together?"

"Yes, if you like. Gracie and Charming will always dance. As one glides, the other must too."

"Bah! Madness!" exclaimed Albert.

*

The young man saw her across the room, walked nervously towards her and asked her to dance. Her heart sank but she did her best to conceal it. Louisa had high hopes for the evening, higher than this fellow anyway, but it wasn't working out as planned. "I'm Abraham. Abe. May I?" he spluttered. "Louisa," she replied, "and yes you may. Thank you. I should warn you, though, I'm not very good at the waltz." "That's OK," he smiled, "neither am I."

Abe held out his hand and Louisa took it. As they stepped out into the music, she looked into his eyes. Immediately she realised that she'd always known him. She couldn't explain this, but she understood somehow that he belonged to her; he was of her as much as, she felt, she must be of him. It was a unity. How could this be? He wasn't her type at all and if her friends had asked her to describe her ideal man, it certainly wouldn't have been Abe.

There was too always too much to say and too little time to say it. Days and weeks became a blur of sharing; of anticipation; of contentment and of hope. Their fear of losing each other increased as they grew closer: the everyday fears of illness, accidents and the million other paranoid worries that is the lot of a young couple in love. But in the background, a greater terror was awake and slithering into their lives. A monster that especially resented both of them.

All too soon, evil would separate them. Only a very few of their families would survive the camps; yet Louisa and Abe did. They had been interned separately, and despite the ghoulish Nazi preoccupation with keeping records, there were none for them. After the liberation, both would leave Poland. Abe settled in Greenock, Scotland and Louisa moved to Ottowa in Canada. Their lives had been altered utterly. Like millions of other surviving souls, they had been scarred and like all those others had made promises that they would never be separated.

*

Abe returned home in the early afternoon. It was warm and he sat in his back garden, novel in hand. Within minutes he was asleep, dreaming. In the dreams he was a young man, whose disciplined body obeyed what it was told to do. He had become that architect, designing cities of the future. Yes, that had been the plan. Louisa would be there too: musician by day and his rock by night but always there, and ever his. In the dream, they were together; walking, talking, fearful, loving or heartbroken, but together. As he dozed off, the book fell from his hands, which were not as strong as they once were. The corner of the back bounced sharply off his right knee before toppling to the grass.

Louisa picked up her little granddaughter and swung her slowly as they danced. Turning awkwardly, she felt a sharp pain in her right knee. "I'm pooped" she laughed, sitting down with little Martha in her lap. "That's ok, granny," Martha replied, hugging her. "Ah my love, you can't fake a hug," laughed Louisa, embracing the little girl tightly.

*

"What keeps these particles – sorry, Gracie and Charming (Albert corrected himself quickly as Niels raised an eyebrow) – moving?"

"But they aren't two particles, Albert. Created together at a moment they are two halves of one particle. As long as they are in the same state, they must do the same thing."

"So, when the state changes?"

"We could speculate that," Niels hesitated, "the wave function collapses."

"Oh come, Niels, let's stick to the script. Wave function? Dancing, not physics! You mean that when Gracie dies, Charming can't feel her anymore?"

"Yes," nodded Niels, "Not in our universe anyway."

"Metaphysics again!" snorted Albert. "Unless we consider The Bridge."

"Which bridge is that?"

"The Einstein-Rosen bridge, my dear friend."

"Aha! So General Theory makes its jazzy appearance at last," laughed Bohr, "staggering all over my ordered quantum world!"

"What an ugly world it is too," continued Einstein. "Collapsing wave functions! When does 'The Cat in the Box' appear?"

Bohr pressed on. "So you fashion a tunnel, Albert?"

"A bridge, yes. Tunnel, wormhole, call it whatever you like. A tunnel with two ends, each at separate points in Spacetime connecting long distances – maybe a billion light years or more – short distances, alternative universes, or different points in time."

"I see," began Bohr, "you are introducing new variables, Albert; a transcendental bijection of the Spacetime continuum, eh?"

"Oh, come now, Niels," scolded Einstein, "and you thought I was the one with no romance in my soul. Transcendental bijections? We've agreed to avoid jargon, haven't we?"

Bohr conceded the point.

*

Louisa had married Simon some years after the war. She had loved him. When he died, she had cried bitter tears and for her it had been yet another wound that could never fully heal.

Metaphorically, she had put away her lost Abe somewhere in a locked box. Experiencing and reliving that earlier life wasn't fair to Simon and she was frightened of it, now that she came to think about it. If she allowed herself to remember Abe, a well of feeling erupted that she couldn't even try to control. If she ever allowed herself to open the box, she didn't know what she'd find.

Abe had never married. There had been many reasons: the war; the camps; what he had seen and heard. He had been lucky to find a home in Scotland and although he didn't become an architect, he had trained as a music teacher and this had given him so much pleasure. His cello playing wasn't first rank but again it was a joy and transported him elsewhere.

"Show me the case, granny," pleaded Martha.

"Oh now, you don't want to see that old thing again."

"Oh I do, granny. Please, please, please."

Anna walked slowly to the corner of the room and opened the case.

"What do you call it again, granny?"

"It's a cello, darling" she smiled.

\*

"So, what does The Bridge do?"

"It functions in an orthodox bridge way," mused Einstein, "connecting two places."

"Well, this sounds a little too convenient," replied Bohr, "a little like the moment in a play when a letter arrives, allowing the narrative to move conveniently from point A to point B."

"I really must protest," replied Einstein. "After all, you are the very man who introduced superposition and entanglement as if they were the most reasonable ideas in the world. So permit me a little latitude."

"I do apologise," replied Niels Bohr, gravely. "Where are you going with this?"

"Well, a foundation for connection. The bridge might permit a connection from one world to another, might it not? Or from one room to another. Let's take René Descartes, for example. He couldn't decide whether he was sleep or awake. He couldn't discriminate between one world and another."

"Yes," interjected Bohr, "but we know that this led to him understanding that although he didn't know where he was, he concluded that he must be somewhere – because of the doubt. I think therefore I am, you know?"

"Absolutely right," continued Einstein. "But for the moment let's at least consider the possibility that our awakening and sleeping worlds are different. If we can agree that premise, then it's also possible that bridges exist, joining those worlds. Furthermore, why should those bridges connect only one person's multiple worlds? Isn't it at least plausible that your entangled pair, your Gracie and Charming, might have a greater expectation of connecting bridges between their worlds than say, you and me?"

"Very much so, Albert."

*

Dozing in the warm afternoon haze, Abe dreamt once more of Louisa. He hadn't meant to but, from time to time, she would appear. It was puzzling because he had tried to blot this out, the memory and the pain. Maybe it was because he was much older now, very tired and with less resolve. He wasn't sure, but for whatever reason, she was an increasingly frequent character in his dreams. She might be young, old, but however she looked, he knew at once that it was her. Was she even alive?

Louisa had had another restless night. She didn't like the night. She feared it, its loneliness and its tendency to encourage irrational thoughts; an unwelcome return of monsters in those depths. She expected that she surely must dream as much as the next old woman, but she could rarely remember any of them. She was also aware – was that the right word? – of Abe. During these dreams, she was spared the pain of his memory; a pain that was all too real during the day. She knew him at once, naturally, and they laughed together, told stories and even had the occasional adventure. He was appearing more often, but curiously with his more frequent visits, he was, in a strange way, becoming less distinct. She couldn't explain that. "What age will I be in Heaven?" she had once asked him. "The age when you first felt love," he had answered.

One stormy night, as an agitated Abe slept feverishly, Louisa had visited him once more. She was holding a book which she solemnly presented to him. Its cover was blank. She smiled – that smile he had long forgotten but now recognised immediately; the one that reached her eyes. He opened the book and inscribed on the inside page were the words, "To my eternal beloved. I may not have found the right book, but I found the right one." Her face broke into a smile. "I remember," he nodded.

"You are never getting rid of me," Louisa laughed. "I

remember a conversation from years ago," she began. "If I died, what should you keep of me? And you said, 'keep whatever you wish, but don't keep me waiting.'"

There was silence; a serene quietness (wherever they were). "Are you ready?" Louisa asked. "Ready?" asked Abe. "Ready to go. I think it's our time." He hugged her and it seemed for a moment that there was now only one person with four arms, four legs and two heads. "It is," he whispered to her. An observer might have called it disintegration but there were no observers and no adequate words to describe what was happening. They had gone.

*

Albert and Niels sat in quiet contemplation, each considering the implications. "So, if one half 'dies' its wave function must collapse?" asked Albert. "Precisely," Niels answered. "What happens to the other half?" continued Albert. Niels, stroked his chin and asked, "Albert, what is half of nothing?" Albert nodded, "Nothing." "Exactly, Albert, yet to anticipate your next question about Gracie and Charming, what is the first law of thermodynamics?"

"Ah, the romance is over. We are back to physics."

"Albert, please?" pressed Niels.

"Energy can neither be created or destroyed, only altered in form," Albert replied.

"Good man, chapter and verse," laughed Niels, clapping his hands. "Albert, as Eddington and Haldane have both put it, the universe is not only stranger than we suppose; it is stranger than we can suppose."

"So, they're still out there, somewhere, somehow?"

"Yes. Bliss; heaven perhaps – who knows? Wouldn't that be just lovely?" Niels drained his glass and Albert put down his pipe. "It would. Indeed, it would."

Then, the two old friends stood, embraced fondly and waltzed around the room. And now they moved as one: with two heads, four arms and four legs, joined in the universal dance.

# THE LAIRD: POSTSCRIPT

Well, who knew what to expect? As before, the Lairdly invite had come unexpectedly. The Laird's ghillie – a woman, incredibly called Gillian, hence her moniker Gillie, the girly ghillie – rapped upon the bothy door. "Six o'clock," she announced, jerking her head up to the castle. "Dinner. Afters too, maybe – if yer lucky." She winked and was gone.

Was this a good sign? A last meal before being exiled or a celebratory feast?

The Laird was standing at the front door in full clan regalia, holding two generous tumblers of the McUisce. "Come in, laddie," he gestured, pushing a full glass in my direction.

I knew better than to drink it. Not yet. He paused and expertly snipped some moss from the wall, plopping it in. "Slàinte!" he announced, raising his glass. "Slàinte," I answered. "Ye'll stay for supper, mon?"

"I'd be delighted, Laird," I replied.

"Aye, I have lots tae ask ye."

In a discreet corner, Fiona, the clan harpist (was every third woman in Scotland called Fiona? I wondered), caressed the strings of the venerable clan harp. But what was that plaintive tune? For the life of me, I couldn't place it, but the slow, driving melody was intoxicating, as indeed was the McUisce, now refilled. I, by this stage, couldn't feel my legs.

The Laird looked over in recognition. "Ye cannie place thon tune, laddie?"

"I'm afraid not, Laird."

"Pinball Wizard, mon!"

Of course.

The Laird motioned to the wall behind him and there, to my surprise, hung a black and white (full-size) portrait photograph. Although the picture was of the man's back, it was unmistakably him. The parka, with plaid fur of course; the target on his back, the Brighton beach backdrop, the outstretched arms with the thumbs up salute.

"Aye, I was a Mod, back in the day, ye ken?"

"Fantastic photograph Laird," I gasped. "Who?...."

"A lad called Bailey took the photo. Wonder wha' became o' him?"

I had so many questions, but knew they'd have to wait.

The Laird motioned me into the banqueting hall. The table was set with the finest clan silverware on display. I had a sudden terrible thought. In all our time together, we'd never broken bread. Did he know I was a vegetarian?

As if reading my mind, he said, "You're a vegetarian, I understand?" I nodded. "Aye. I ken. Gillie, ma ghillie has done her homework."

"Really?"

"Aye, her years in SIS weren't entirely a waste."

"SIS? You mean…?" I spluttered.

"Aye, laddie. Some class o' spook. Foreign climes only, o' course. England and so on."

The Laird seemed to shudder at the very thought. Of course, a faraway place. He pressed on. "I admire that, mon. My time with the Yogi lads in India. Ye got tae keep an open mind."

I sat facing him. From nowhere, it seemed, Gillian had materialised bearing a decanter of white wine. The Laird regarded it with fierce pride. "Something a little special, laddie. From the vines on ma southern slopes."

"Microclimate," purred the girly ghillie into my right ear by way of explanation. "Large one?" she added – a tad mischievously, I thought.

"Thank you," I replied.

Course after sumptuous course followed. With each, The Laird dissected every story. I shouldn't have been surprised about his knowledge of quantum mechanics, philosophy, Celtic folklore and all the rest.

When the business and banquet had concluded, the Laird rose and shook my hand. "Goodnight, mon," he said. "Gillie will show you back to the bothy. Enjoy the rest of yer evening," he chuckled, his eyes twinkling below bushy arched eyebrows.

And once again, from the shadows, Gillian was suddenly there: a vision in plaid, with night goggles in her hands.

"But before ye go," the Laird added, "I have one last question."

"Yes, Laird?"

"Ha' ye got a sequel in ye, laddie?"